MARGERY MO'S MAGIC ISLAND

Scholastic Children's Books
Scholastic Publications Ltd
7-9 Pratt Street, London NW1 0AE, UK

Scholastic Inc
730 Broadway, New York, NY 10003, USA

Scholastic Canada Ltd
123 Newkirk Road, Richmond Hill
Ontario, Canada L4C 3G5

Ashton Scholastic Pty Ltd
PO Box 579, Gosford, New South Wales
Australia

Ashton Scholastic Ltd
Private Bag 1, Penrose, Auckland
New Zealand

First published in the UK 1992 by André Deutsch Children's Books
an imprint of Scholastic Children's Books

Text copyright © 1992 by Margaret Donaldson
Illustrations copyright © 1992 by Debi Gliori

ISBN: 0 590 54057 2

Typeset by Rapid Reprographics, London
Printed by in Hong Kong by Paramount Printing Group Limited

MARGERY MO'S MAGIC ISLAND

Margaret Donaldson
Illustrated by Debi Gliori

André Deutsch Children's Books

4

Margery Mo and her big brother Joe were sitting at the table, drawing pictures. Margery Mo drew her mummy going for a walk with Chu-Chu. Joe drew a space-man.

When Joe had finished his drawing he began to read a book. Then Mo had an idea. She thought she would draw a little space-girl walking beside Joe's space-man. She did it just for fun, but when Joe looked round and saw what she was doing he was very angry.

"You've spoiled my picture!" he shouted. "You've made a dreadful mess on it!"

"It's not a dreadful mess, it's a space-girl," Mo said. "And it's a *nice* space-girl," she added.

But Joe was still angry. He shouted at her again:

"You've spoiled my drawing! You're always making trouble!"

He grabbed the drawing and tore it into little bits.

"Now *you've* spoiled my space-girl," Mo said. "And she was a *nice* space-girl."

Joe swept his hand across the table. All the bits of paper flew up in the air then fell on the floor.

"Mummy will make you pick those up," Mo said. But all the same she felt like crying, so she decided to go and look for Chu-Chu. As she went out of the door, Joe shouted "Trouble-maker!"

Mo found Chu-Chu and sat in a corner hugging him. But she still felt like crying so she decided to go to her magic island. She could go there any time she liked. All she had to do was shut her eyes and say some magic words, then she was there. (But she never told anyone what the magic words were. They were a secret.)

When Mo reached the island the first person she saw
was Princess Poppadom. She nearly always saw
Princess Poppadom first, because Princess Poppadom
lived in a tall tree and you could hardly miss her. The
tree had golden leaves, fit for a princess.

"Hullo, Mo!" said the princess. "Nice to see you
again. I expect you have a question to ask, haven't
you?"

"Yes I have," said Mo. "The question is: have you
got a make-trouble on the island?"

Princess Poppadom looked very puzzled.

"I really don't know," she said. "What's a make-trouble?"

"It's someone who makes trouble of course," Mo told her.

"Ah!" said the princess. "You mean a trouble-maker. Yes, of course we've got one of those. We've got one of nearly everything on this island."

"Well, can you please find the make-trouble – I mean the trouble-maker?" Mo asked.
Princess Poppadom swung her legs about until the golden leaves made a tinkling noise.

"Whatever do you want him for?" she said. "He's not very popular, you know. Most people stay away from him."

13

Margery Mo sat down on a big stone and wondered how to explain. Then she said:

"What I want to know is . . . is how to make trouble and so . . . and so then how *not* to make trouble if I don't want to."
Princess Poppadom opened her eyes wide.

"Sensible child," she said. "Everyone should know that. Why didn't I think of it before? I'll send for the Trouble-maker at once."

She sat up straight and shouted in a loud voice:
　　　"Come out, come out, wherever you are,
　　　Trouble-maker, near or far!"
And suddenly there he was, right in front of Mo, a
wispy, waspy sort of fellow, very thin. He must have
been near, not far, or else it was magic. Perhaps he had
been hiding behind one of the trees all the time,
listening to everything.

"What do you want then, your Highness?" asked the Trouble-maker. (And she really was a very high Highness sitting up there in her tree.)

"This child wants to ask you a question," said the Princess. "Go ahead, Mo. Ask him." And she wiggled her legs again so as to make the tinkling noise. She liked doing it.

Mo looked at the Trouble-maker.

"It will be an easy question for you to answer, Mr. Trouble-maker," she said politely. "I just want to know how to make trouble."

The Trouble-maker smiled, but it wasn't a nice smile. Then he said:

"Aha!" – and again, "Aha!" and again, "Aha!"

Mo waited for more, but nothing came. He was quite silent, just smiling his not-nice smile.

"But how do you do it?" she said at last. "You haven't told me."

"Of course I haven't," said the Trouble-maker. "What did you expect? That's my secret. We've all got secrets, haven't we?"

Princess Poppadom nodded her head and looked very wise.

"He's right, you know," she said. "We've all got secrets. I've got one." And she began to recite a poem:

> "I sleep up here all the year round
> And never, never fall to the ground."

Mo was puzzled.

"That's not a secret," she said.
The Princess laughed.

"The secret is how I manage to do it," she explained. "Nobody knows except me."

Margery Mo remembered the magic words she used for getting to the island. They were her secret. So it was fair for the Trouble-maker to have a secret too.

"All right, Mr Trouble-maker," she said, sighing a little. "Keep your secret, then."
The Trouble-maker smiled his not-nice smile again.

"Tell you what I *will* do," he said. "I'll show you my trouble-making factory. I'll show you the piles and piles of trouble that I've made. I have enough trouble in store to last the island for years and years."

Mo didn't believe him. Trouble's not like that, she thought. It's not *stuff*, like sugar. But she wasn't quite sure. She wanted to see if he really had a factory.

"Come on, little girl," said the Trouble-maker. "Follow me."

He was already walking away into the trees.

Mo didn't know what to do. Then she felt something fluttering close to her ear. It was Blue Butterfly, and she was whispering:

"No, no! Don't go, don't go!"

Mo looked at the Trouble-maker, who was still smiling his not-nice smile.

"Why not?" she whispered to Blue Butterfly. "Why not?"

"Because trouble is tricky, sticky stuff. If you get into it, it's hard to get out again. Don't go, don't go! Say no, say no!"

Margery Mo looked at the Trouble-maker.

"No!" she said very loudly. "I won't go with you." She waved to Princess Poppadom.

"Thank you for helping me," she said. "I'm going now. See you soon!"
And she shut her eyes quickly and said the magic words for going home.

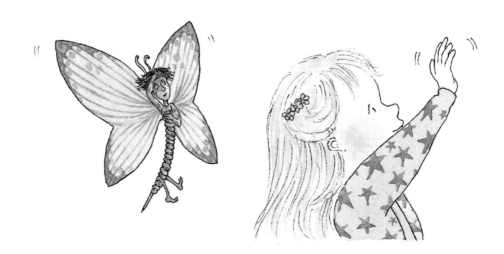

When she opened her eyes again, she was back with Chu-Chu, sitting on the floor in the corner. And Joe was looking down at her.

"Would you like to come and draw a new space-girl?" he said. "I'll draw a space-man walking beside her, if you like."

Mo was pleased. She got up and they went into the kitchen together.